ABOUT THE AUTHOR

Angie Sage trained as an artist and began her career illustrating books, but she always wanted to write. She has two daughters, Laurie and Lois, whose wicked sense of humour finds its way into her stories. She also loves sailing, the sea and Cornwall.

For little sister Lois

Ellie's Slugbucket

Angie Sage

Hodder
Children's
Books

a division of Hodder Headline plc

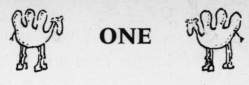

ONE

Today was going to be a good day. It was going to be a *great* day, the day when at last I had someone else to play with. Today was the day that the new people next door were moving in.

Ever since my best friend moved away from the flat upstairs, it has just been me, Ellie and Harold the rat. If you offered me the choice between Harold the rat and my small sister Ellie, I'd choose Harold the rat any day. But no one *has* offered me the choice so I'm stuck with both of them.

Harold was asleep in his cage and Ellie was putting the finishing touches to her slug holiday village. She had collected at least twenty slugs in her slug bucket, and now the slugs were going to have a holiday of a lifetime. Well, that's what Ellie said, anyway.

'Slugs don't have holidays,' I pointed out in my helpful big sister voice.

Ellie made one of her 'get lost' faces, '*My* slugs have holidays. They are having a holiday right now. So there.' She dropped a small slug on top of what could have been a sunbed and plopped another one into what was probably a swimming-pool.

'Eurgh,' I said. I had caught sight of the slug bucket and felt a bit sick.

Suddenly a loud voice rang out from next door. They had arrived! I zoomed across to the hedge in the front garden and peered over. It didn't look too good to me. A spiky-looking woman wearing pointy pink glasses got out of a very smart car, followed by a small boy wearing big glasses that made him look a bit like an owl.

Ellie rushed up 'Let me see.' She elbowed me out of the way and stood on tip-toe to have a good look. She promptly fell into the hedge.

'That's what comes of pushing people,' I told her as I very kindly pulled her out. The pointy pink glasses stared at us disapprovingly. Then their owner grabbed hold of the boy's hand and whisked him inside.

Ellie and I stared through the hole that she'd made in the hedge. There was plenty to see. Two huge removal vans turned up and streams of removal people started carrying in vases and pots. There were fat pots, thin pots, tall pots and small pots.

'That's horrible,' said Ellie as a large brown pot with three fish stuck on the top sailed past us.

'But that's even worse,' I giggled as a huge green elephant pot with glowing red eyes went by. 'I wouldn't like to bump into that in the dark.'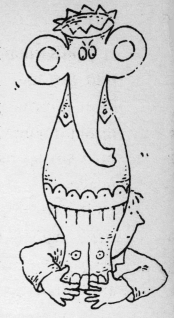

'Eugh,' agreed Ellie.

I didn't see the small boy with glasses until later when I was hanging around the fence in the back garden trying to get away from the slug holiday village. Suddenly I heard a loud screech from an upstairs window next door. It was the pointy pink glasses again.

'Humphrey! Come away from the fence *dear*. I don't want you talking to those people in the flats.'

Just as I was wondering what a Humphrey was, I heard a loud whisper from the other side of the fence. 'Hello,' it said, 'who are you?'

I peered over. The whisper belonged to the small boy with glasses. He didn't look too bad, I thought to myself. Better than Harold the rat, anyway.

'I'm Kate.' I said. 'Who are you then?'

'I'm Humphrey Hogbin.'

'You're joking,' I said.

'No.' He looked down at his feet. Poor kid, I thought, fancy being stuck with a name like that.

Suddenly Ellie was there beside me. 'Is that really your name?' she giggled. 'Humphrey, like the camel?'

'What camel?' asked Humphrey, blinking his eyes behind his specs.

'You *know*,' said Ellie, 'the one with three humps.'

Humphrey blinked again. 'Three humps?'

'Humphrey! Come inside NOW!' the voice shouted. It sounded really cross.

'That's my mum. Must go,' muttered Humphrey, and ran off.

Ellie stared over the fence and watched him disappear into the house next door.

'You shouldn't make fun of people's names,' I told her. 'It's rude.' Sometimes you have to say things like that if you have a little sister. If Ellie is your little sister, you have to say things like that quite often.

'Shuddup,' said Ellie and went back to her slug holiday village.

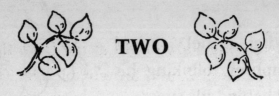

TWO

Another thing about having a small sister is that you need somewhere to go where she can't get you. So that's where I took myself off to, my sister-proof tree. It happens to look out over the front of the house next door and I thought I might catch a glimpse of Humphrey through the windows. Maybe his mum was holding him prisoner or something. Maybe she wasn't his mum at all.

I climbed right up to the top branch and pulled up the rope behind me. Then I opened the old ice cream carton that I keep up there and dug out my telescope. It's only a plastic one that I won on a hook-a-duck stall but it works really well. I pointed the telescope at next door and waited.

The first thing I saw was *revolting*. A huge

monster slug stared right at me from the middle of a pink and brown splodge. The pink and brown splodge was Ellie's hand

and it was about to ring next door's doorbell. I put down the telescope and stared. It was too late to stop Ellie now.

Ellie pressed the doorbell and Humphrey Hogbin's mother opened the door. She looked at Ellie and sort of staggered back a bit. I know how she felt.

'Yes. What do you want, little girl?' she said in snappy voice.

'I have come to give Hump-free a present,' piped up Ellie, 'because of what I said about the camel.'

Humphrey's mum took another step back. She looked at Ellie in the way that you look at those really big hairy spiders when they scuttle out of your boots. Then Humphrey appeared.

'Here you are,' said Ellie. She pushed her pudgy little fist towards Humphrey and dropped the slug into his hand.

Humphrey's mum screamed, turned to run and tripped over the doormat. I heard a loud crash as something hit the floor and smashed.

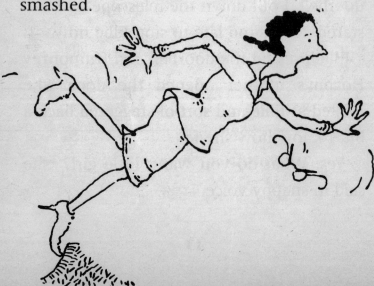

Ellie took no notice. 'That's Egbert,' she told Humphrey. 'He's my best slug. I'm sorry about the camel. It's a nice name really.' She turned and wandered off down the path, leaving Humphrey staring at a muddy slug and Mrs Hogbin lying flat out on the floor.

That's Ellie for you. She leaves a trail of disasters wherever she goes.

Later that evening when we were having supper Mum said, 'I had a visit from our new neighbour. I think she's a little, er, strange. She rambled on about smashed priceless Chinese vases and slugs. I do hope she's not going to be a nuisance.'

'That's what Kate said *I* was,' mumbled Ellie through a mouthful of chips.

'Well, she shouldn't have,' said Mum. 'Anyway, talking of nuisances, that rat needs his cage cleaning out.' Mum looked at me. 'It's your turn Kate.'

I groaned. I hate cleaning out Harold's

cage. He's Ellie's rat too, but Mum says she's too little to do his cage properly, so me and Mum share it.

I was about to moan and stomp off when two surprising things happened. The first one was Ellie saying, 'I'm big now. Harold wants me to clean out his cage. Can I, Mum. Please please, can I *can I*?'

The second one was Mum saying, 'All right then, Ellie. If you're very careful.'

It's strange how things turn out sometimes. Especially if Ellie has anything to do with them. It was even stranger the next morning.

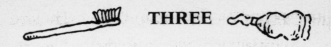

THREE

Ellie was up early next morning. She is always up early and the first thing she does is to come and jump on my bed and pretend that she is a wild elephant. For some reason Ellie thinks this is really funny.

Well, this morning there was no wild elephant. She got out of bed so quietly that it woke me up. I am not used to Ellie trying to be quiet. I pretended to be asleep and watched her creep out of our bedroom. Then I threw on an old jumper over my pyjamas and followed her.

Ellie was in the kitchen trying to open a packet of digestive biscuits.

'You're not allowed to eat biscuits before breakfast,' I said.

Ellie spun round and looked at me

guiltily. 'They're not for me, silly. They're for...' She stopped and stuffed the biscuits back in the cupboard.

'They're for *who*?' I asked. I smelt a rat. Then I thought, RAT. I shot a glance over to Harold's cage. At first I thought that Harold had gone strangely lumpy and I went over and took a closer look. Curled up inside  Harold's cage was one of Ellie's socks stuffed with – I picked the sock up and shook it. Bits of shredded up newspaper fell out.

'Where's Harold?' I demanded, waving the saggy sock in the air.

Ellie looked sulky. 'Dunno,' she muttered.

'You've lost Harold! I knew you would. I bet you let him out of his cage.'

'He gets bored in his cage. So I let him run around a bit while I cleaned it. I thought he'd come back,' sniffed Ellie, 'but he didn't.'

'Of course he didn't,' I said crossly. 'He's just a stupid rat.'

'He's *not* stupid,' said Ellie.

'Mum's going to be really cross,' I told her.

'I know,' Ellie's bottom lip quivered. That's a bad sign, it means big tears next, and I'm not very good at getting Ellie to stop once she gets going.

'Look,' I said, picking up the old sock and stuffing the newspaper back into it. 'Mum won't notice the difference. Put the sock back in until we find Harold.'

Ellie put the sock back into the cage and covered it over with Harold's bedding, then she closed the door quietly as if she was afraid of waking the sock up.

'I liked Harold,' sniffed Ellie. 'He liked me too.' She wandered off to clean her teeth. *Clean her teeth*! Ellie must be feeling bad, I thought.

Ellie was quiet all morning. She disappeared into the garden and carried on messing about with her slugs. The more intelligent slugs had escaped from the slug bucket in the night. Ellie put the stupid ones who were left into the holiday village and went off to catch some more.

I decided to look for Harold. I know I may have said some not very nice things about Harold earlier, but I thought it might be a good idea to get him back before Mum found out that he'd run away. Mum had gone off to the shops so I decided to start looking in her bedroom. I looked under the bed and on top of the wardrobe, then I thought I heard a rustling behind the curtains. I dashed over and looked on the windowsill, but it was only the breeze blowing the curtains about. Then something caught my eye.

Mum's bedroom window looks out over the Hogbins' front garden. There was a small black van coming into the driveway. I watched Mrs Hogbin run out to it, looking very jumpy. Two men wearing boiler suits and carrying black cases got out of the van. Mrs Hogbin sort of pushed them up the pathway and into the house.

It was then that I saw the sign on the side of the van. It said:

Now I knew where Harold was. Harold the rat was next door with Mrs Hogbin and two rat-catchers. I knew something else too: Harold the rat was in danger.

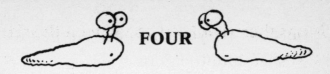

FOUR

I tore down the stairs and out of the house. Somehow I had to rescue Harold before it was too late. I decided to creep through a hole in the fence in the back garden and see if I could get into the Hogbins' house. It was risky, but I couldn't think of anything else.

I saw Ellie and her slug bucket hanging around by the garden fence. The last thing I wanted was Ellie tagging along with me, so I crawled through the patch of rough grass that no one bothers to cut.

'SEEN YOU!' yelled Ellie triumphantly. She rushed into the grass.

'Whaddyou playing?' she asked. 'Can I play too?'

'No. Go away,' I whispered loudly.

Ellie scuttled off towards the house crying 'Mum, Mum, Kate won't let me play with her. MUM!'

Can you believe it? There I am trying to sort out the mess that Ellie has got us (well, Harold) into and she goes and makes things even worse. I rushed after her and stopped her from grabbing Mum who had just got back from the shops.

'Oi, let go of me!' yelled Ellie.

Mum put down four large bags and looked cross. 'Can't I leave you two alone for five minutes without you fighting?' she asked.

''S'all right, Mum. I'll let Ellie play. Come on, then,' I hissed at Ellie, 'quick.'

I decided I had to tell Ellie about Harold. As soon as Mum had gone in, I said, 'Harold's next door with Mrs Hogbin and two rat-catchers.'

'I know,' said Ellie.

'What?'

'I *know*,' said Ellie as though I was stupid. 'Hump-free told me. I just been telling him about Harold. Hump-free says his mummy saw Harold this morning. Hump-free says rats make his mummy go funny. Hump-free says-'

'Oh, bother what Humphrey says.'

Ellie took no notice. 'Hump-free says that he'll meet us in the top flat in ten minutes. You coming or what?' she asked.

Well! How does Ellie do it? How does she always manage to keep one step ahead? For example, how come she always gets the red jam tarts? Because she puts sticky finger prints on them when they're still in the box and then no one else wants to eat them, that's how. So what had she been up to this time? That's what I wanted to know.

Ellie went off, swinging her squirming slug bucket. I let her get safely ahead, then I followed her in.

Ellie and I live in the middle flat in a big old house. It's half a house really, because it's joined on to the Hogbins' house. Their house isn't divided into flats so Humphrey has lots of space to play in. But Ellie and I don't do too badly because no one minds if we play in the empty flats in our big old house either. That's because the caretaker is really nice.

As I followed Ellie's thumpy footsteps up to the top flat I wondered how Humphrey thought he was going to be able to meet us. I didn't give much for his chances of escaping from Mrs Hogbin and the rat-catchers. Then I thought of poor Harold. 'Hurry *up*, Ellie! We've got to get Harold,' I puffed.

'I *am* hurrying. Stop bossing me,' said Ellie.

The top flat was very quiet and empty. I hadn't

been up there since my best friend left, and it looked bigger than I remembered it. There was no sign of Humphrey anywhere.

'You must have got it wrong,' I told Ellie. 'How could Humphrey meet us here anyway?'

'He could. So there,' said Ellie unhelpfully. Ellie will never let on that she might have made a mistake. Not even a big one, like eating my chocolate buttons as well as hers.

I was just about to go back downstairs when something really weird happened. I don't usually jump two metres up in the air and scream, but I did then: 'Aargh! Humphrey!'

Humphrey walked through the wall. Just like you see on those ghost stories late at night when you're not meant to be watching.

Ellie wasn't a bit surprised, which made me suspicious. 'Hello, Hump-free,' she said, '*Kate* didn't think you were coming.'

Humphrey blinked through his glasses and grinned. Ellie grinned too. In fact they both looked rather smug. It's always irritating when  people look smug, usually because they know something that you don't. So I said, 'OK, what's going on here?'

'I found it yesterday,' said Humphrey. 'Isn't it great?'

'Found what. *What's* great?' I asked him rather crossly.

'That.' Humphrey pointed to the wall. Then Ellie skipped over to where he was pointing and pushed hard on the wall. A small door swung open. I decided not to appear too impressed, although it was really exciting. I sauntered over and peered through. I couldn't see much. 'What's in there, then?'

'My house,' said Humphrey, happily. 'It goes into my attic.'

'We can go and see Hump-free whenever we want to,' piped up Ellie, 'without asking his mummy first.'

A secret door. That was the best thing

that had happened in a long time, but there was something I still wanted to know about.

'How come you knew about it?' I asked Ellie. She didn't answer. 'You'll have to tell me.'

'Why?'

'Because...because otherwise I'll tell Mum about Harold.'

'You wouldn't.'

'I would.'

Ellie got very sulky. 'Hump-free can tell you if he wants.'

'I found the door last night,' said Humphrey. 'When I opened it Ellie was here cleaning out Harold's cage.'

'Why did you come up *here* to clean out the cage?' I asked Ellie.

'I'm allowed up here,' said Ellie sulkily. 'I like it up here. So does Harold. And there are no bossy big sisters telling me how to clean his cage out properly.'

I was about to tell her that I am most definitely *not* a bossy big sister and she shouldn't be so rude, when Humphrey said the most amazing thing.

'Harold woke my Mum up this morning.'

'What?' I gasped.

'He woke my Mum up. I heard Mum screaming and yelling. When I went in to see what it was, there he was, sitting on her pillow eating the rest of the biscuit that she has with her cocoa.'

'Wow...' breathed Ellie. 'What kind of biscuit was it?'

'Ellie!' I said. 'Never mind about biscuits, what about Harold? We've got to rescue him. There isn't much time.'

'Come on,' said Humphrey, 'we must find him before the rat-catchers do.'

With that, Humphrey pushed open the secret door and Ellie and I followed him into the Hogbins' house.

FIVE

We all crept through Humphrey's attic as quietly as we could, which, for Ellie, was about as quiet as a small hippo.

'Shhh...' I turned to whisper and then I noticed something horrible. Ellie was bringing her slug bucket along and it was full to the brim with slimy, squirming slugs. 'Eurgh. Leave that slug bucket behind, Ellie. Those slugs are revolting.'

'No they're not. They're lovely. It rained last night so they're all fat and juicy and – '

'Oh stop it, *please*. You're making me feel sick.'

Ellie didn't say anything else, but she didn't put the slug bucket down either.

So Humphrey, me, Ellie and the overflowing slug bucket crept out of the Hogbins' attic and down the lovely fluffy pink stair carpet of the attic stairs. Bits of mud dropped off the bucket and a couple of slugs saw their chance and made a break for it. We kept going until we got to the landing.

'Wow,' whispered Ellie. I knew what she meant. Humphrey's house was so *clean*. It was also stuffed full of those china pots and vases that we had watched coming in the day before. I looked at Ellie clumping along in her big wellie boots and just hoped that she would miss the most expensive ones.

A gruff rat-catcher voice drifted up from the basement. 'No sign of the little blighter here, missus. We'll try the next floor now. Flush 'im out in no time we will, don't you worry.'

'Harold!' squeaked Ellie in a sort of strangled whisper.

'Don't worry, Ellie, we'll find him,' I said. The last thing we needed was an upset Ellie.

'I *seed* him!' whispered Ellie. 'I seed his tail go round that door.' She pointed to a door that was half open on the other side of the landing.

'Quick then!' said Humphrey, diving towards the half open door. Ellie and I did not need telling twice, we piled in after Humphrey and Ellie slammed the door behind us.

'Shh!' I hissed at Ellie as the rat-catchers thumped around in the hallway downstairs.

The room was stuffed full of cardboard boxes. Some were empty and some were still full of Mrs Hogbin's bits and pieces.

There was no sign of Harold anywhere. It was a rat paradise, full of hundreds of interesting little rat hiding-places.

'He could be anywhere,' sighed Humphrey as he turned over an empty box.

'I wish I had a biscuit,' said Ellie.

'It will be lunch soon. You'll just have to wait.' I told her.

'Not for me. For *Harold*.' Ellie gave me a funny look. 'Hump-free's mummy has biscuits in her bedroom. Go and get one of your mummy's biscuits, Hump-free.' Humphrey gave Ellie a funny look. I could tell that he'd never met anything like her before.

'Er, OK,' he said and slipped out to Mrs Hogbin's bedroom.

'You shouldn't boss Humphrey around like that,' I told Ellie when Humphrey had gone. Someone has to tell her otherwise she's going to start bossing *everyone* around. Even me.

'Why not?' asked Ellie.

I didn't have time to answer because at that moment Humphrey and a packet of biscuits shot back into the room.

'*Hide,*' he whispered loudly. '*They're coming up here!*'

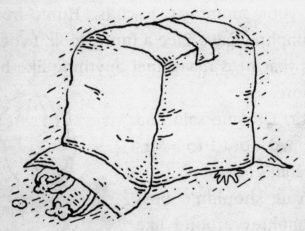

We hid. Humphrey and I squeezed behind a big box marked 'This way up' and Ellie shot inside a smaller box in the middle of the room.

Then I saw Harold.

He was sitting on top of a box in a far corner happily scratching behind his ears and cleaning his nose. I was about to dash out and get him when the door flew open.

In marched Mrs Hogbin and the rat-catchers.

SIX

Suddenly everything in the room went quiet. It was so quiet that I was sure Mrs Hogbin could hear us all breathing. I was also sure that any minute now Ellie would cough or giggle or do something silly. But she didn't, she was as quiet as a mouse – or a rat. Harold the rat was pretty quiet too. He must have known that something was going on because he just sat on top of that box and kept completely still.

''E's in 'ere missus,' said Catchem or Bashem. 'I can smell 'im. I can smell a rat. Ha ha.' I suppose he thought that was a joke.

Mrs Hogbin squeaked nervously. 'I think I'll wait outside while you, er…'

'Bash 'im on the 'ead?' chortled the other rat-catcher. 'Now, missus, we don't want

42

'im escaping when you open the door. You better stay put.'

Mrs Hogbin stayed put.

The rat-catchers started prowling through the room while Harold sat on top of his box and watched them. His little whiskers were quite still as he pretended to be a small rat statue. I closed my eyes, I couldn't bear to watch any more – in a few minutes Harold would be history.

It's funny how when you close your eyes you often hear sounds more clearly. I was sure I could hear a scuffling, scratching noise. At first I thought it was the rat-catchers making their way across the room but I could hear a weird moaning sound too. And then —

'AARGH!' That was Mrs Hogbin. I knew a Mrs Hogbin scream anywhere. 'AARGH!' She did it again and then yelled out, 'It's *moving*! I can see it moving! It's a ghost. A ghost!'

Well, I had to open my eyes at that. I peered around the edge of the box and a strange sight met my eyes. Ellie's box was slowly moving across the room and inside it Ellie was making some very spooky moaning noises. Mrs Hogbin was staring at it. She had gone very white, her eyes were wide open and looked as though they

44

might pop out of her head at any moment.

Then Ellie started the scratching sounds. Scratch...scritch...scratch...on the sides of the box.

'It's trying to get out. *The ghost is trying to get out.*' Mrs Hogbin stood rooted to the spot, but the rat-catchers had had enough.

'We don't catch no ghosts. That ain't our job. We're off, missus.' They shot out of the door and slammed it shut behind them, leaving Mrs Hogbin alone, or so she thought.

'Don't leave me in here on my own!' yelled Mrs Hogbin. 'Wait for me!' She wrenched the door open and tore out after them.

I heard three pairs of feet clattering down the stairs, the front door slam and then the sound of the rat-catchers trying to get their van started.

Humphrey and I pushed our way through the piles of boxes to the window just in time to see the rat-catchers' van skid out of the drive with the tyres spinning. It shot off up the road, closely followed by Mrs Hogbin who was running faster than I would have thought possible in those funny shoes that she wears.

'I hope she's all right,' said Humphrey.

'She'll be OK,' I said. 'I expect she's gone to see a friend or something. That's what my mum does when she goes a bit funny.'

Ellie emerged from her box giggling. 'That was fun. I was a good ghost, wasn't I?'

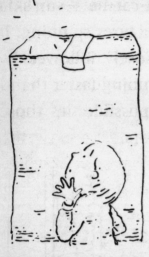

'Yes, very good, Ellie. Now let's grab Harold and get out of here before Mrs Hogbin starts to wonder what was really under that box.' I looked up at the top of Harold's box, but he had gone. Trust Harold.

We looked through all the boxes, but Harold had done his disappearing act again. I climbed up to have a look above the window and saw Mum out in the garden. She was looking cross and shouting, 'Ellie! Kate! Where are you? LUNCH-TIME!'

I had no idea how long we had been looking for Harold but it must have been much longer than I thought.

'Come on, Ellie. We'd better go.'

'But what about Harold? We can't go till we've got Harold.' Ellie stuck out her bottom lip and looked stubborn.

'I'll look for Harold, Ellie,' said Humphrey. 'You'd better go and have your lunch.'

'All right, Hump-free,' said Ellie, as good as gold. For a moment I wondered why and then I found out. 'Can I have the biscuits please, Hump-free?' Ellie asked.

Humphrey handed over the biscuits, 'There you are Ellie. Now go and have your lunch – *please*.' Humphrey sounded rather frazzled. Could it have been anything to do with Ellie?

I shoved Ellie across the landing towards the attic stairs while Humphrey carried on pushing the boxes around. Ellie fished a couple of biscuits out of the packet.

'Put them back.' I told her.

'Stop bossing me,' Ellie said as she scrunched the biscuits up in her sticky

hands. Then she dropped them on the soft pink carpet.

'Ellie don't!' I whispered. Then I saw what she was doing. Ellie was laying a biscuit trail for Harold to follow. She sprinkled the biscuit crumbs all the way back up the stairs, across the two attics and down into our flat, right up to the door of Harold's cage.

'Now,' she whispered as we sat down to our fish fingers, 'all we've got to do is wait for Harold to turn up.'

Someone turned up, but it wasn't Harold.

SEVEN

The person who turned up was Mrs Hogbin.

Mum had just cast a glance at Harold's cage with the sock still curled up happily inside it, and said, 'Harold's very sleepy today,' when there was a very long ring on our doorbell. It went on and on.

'Bother,' said Mum as she got up to go downstairs. Ellie and I breathed a sigh of relief – neither of us wanted to chat to Mum about the sock's sleeping habits.

Mum was gone a long time. Ellie had got through about half a bottle of tomato ketchup by the time she came back. Mum sat down at the table and pushed away her cold fishfingers.

'That was Mrs Hogbin,' she said rather quietly.

Whoops, I thought to myself. Ellie made a funny face at me across the table.

'Have either of you met Mrs Hogbin?' Mum asked.

'Er, well, sort of. I mean Ellie did. But not for long, did you Ellie?' I kicked Ellie under the table to tell her not to say too much.

'Stoppit,' said Ellie. 'She's kicking me, Mum.'

'What?' said Mum. She was still thinking about Mrs Hogbin.

'What did you think of Mrs Hogbin, Ellie? I mean, was she all right?' Mum whispered this last bit as though Mrs Hogbin was about to rush in and jump on us.

'No, she's not all right,' declared Ellie, 'She's a horrible bat.'

'You mean horrible *old* bat,' I said.

'There's no need to be rude about her,' said Mum. 'I'm sure she can't help it, but she wouldn't stop talking about plagues of rats and ghosts in boxes. I think the strain of moving house has been too much for her.'

'What did she come round for then, Mum?' I asked. I was still sure that Mrs Hogbin had come over to complain about

Harold, or Ellie, or the biscuit crumbs, or the muddy pink carpet or – well I could think of quite a few things that she might want to complain about.

'Oh,' said Mum, 'she wanted to know where the vicar lived. She seems to think that he'll come round and get rid of the ghosts. Meanwhile, just to be on the safe side, I don't want either of you going near Mrs Hogbin, OK?'

'OK Mum,' we said.

It was getting late when Ellie remembered something rather important. Well, something rather important to Ellie, that is. We were sitting quietly while Mum was in the kitchen writing some letters, when Ellie suddenly went, 'Ooh' and clapped her hands over her mouth.

'What now?' I sighed. I was reading a really good story and I had just got to the exciting bit.

'Slug bucket!' yelped Ellie. '*Slug bucket*. I left it at Hump-free's house!'

EIGHT

'Where *exactly*,' I asked Ellie crossly, 'did you leave your horrible slug bucket?' I could see that Ellie was trying to think. She looked up at her eyebrows and chewed the neck of her T-shirt.

'When I seed Harold,' she said slowly, 'I put my bucket down by that horrible green elephant pot. Then we ran after Harold and I didn't pick my bucket up.'

'So your slug bucket is still on Mrs Hogbin's landing? Oh great.'

Ellie looked sulky and stared at the floor. 'I want to get my slug bucket,' she said, 'I want to get my slug bucket NOW.'

It was beginning to get dark and I did not like the idea of going up to the top flat at all. The electricity had been turned off up there so it would be really dark and creepy.

As for going down into the Hogbins' without Humphrey, well I definitely didn't like that idea.

'The slugs will just have to wait until Humphrey comes over with Harold,' I told Ellie.

'But that could be ages,' wailed Ellie. 'My slugs are all alone in that horrible house with no one to talk to.'

'Slugs don't talk, Ellie,' I said, trying my patient big sister voice. It didn't work.

'Suppose Hump-free never finds Harold, I'll never ever see my slugs again.' Ellie always exaggerates.

'Of course he'll find Harold,' I told her. 'You're being silly. And your slugs have probably all gone to sleep by now. Now go away and let me finish my story.'

Ellie stuck her tongue out at me and then wandered off. I settled down and carried on reading.

It was a while later when I noticed how

quiet it was. It was the kind of quiet that you only get when Ellie is not around. All I could hear was the sound of Mum shuffling

paper in the kitchen and the whooshing sound that the gas fire makes. I got up and went to see if Ellie was sulking in our bedroom, but there was no sign of her.

Then I heard the tell-tale creak of a floorboard right above my head. Someone was in the top flat and I had a strange feeling that it was Ellie.

creak creak

Bother, I thought. I wondered if I could just leave her there, but I knew I couldn't. I went to get my torch.

Of course my torch had gone; it was already up in the top flat with Ellie. So I had to climb up those creepy, dusty stairs in the dark. When I got to the top it was a little bit lighter. The moon was rising and it shone through the skylight, lighting up the funny old cooker and the grubby sink.

The secret door was half open and beyond it I could see an Ellie-shaped shadow. I crept through the door and came out into the Hogbins' attic.

There was Ellie sitting very still at the top of the stairs, holding my torch. She hadn't even noticed me.

I know I shouldn't have, but I couldn't resist it. Anyway, she *had* stuck her tongue out at me earlier. I crept up behind her.

'BOO!' I said.

NINE

'I knew you'd do that,' whispered Ellie grumpily. 'I've been waiting for you for ages.'

I sat down next to her. 'What are you doing? Are you going down to get your horrible slug bucket?'

'It's not horrible. I *am* going to get it,' whispered Ellie. 'I told you, I've been waiting for you.'

The stairs and the landing in the Hogbins'
house were very dark. I didn't like the look
of them at all. 'I don't think we should go
down there, Ellie. Not without Humphrey.'

'*I want my slug bucket,*' said Ellie. '*And I'm
going to get it. So there.*'

I stopped trying to argue, 'Oh, go on
then,' I said. 'I'll sit here while you nip
down and get it. I'll be the look-out.'

Ellie looked unimpressed. 'You're scared,'
she said.

'No I'm not.'

'Well, come on then.' Ellie stood up and started to tip-toe down the first fluffy pink steps into the Hogbins' house. I followed her.

We reached the landing. It was really creepy and I wished Ellie would hurry up and get her stupid slug bucket.

'Can you see it anywhere?' I whispered.

'No, it must be behind the elephant.' Ellie waved her torch at the huge green

elephant pot. Its beady red eyes glinted in the torch light and stared down at us. It reminded me of Mrs Hogbin. I shivered, it was creepy.

And then I heard something *really* creepy. A low, weird moany voice reciting a poem or something. I thought it was coming from the box-room where poor Harold was.

'Can you hear that?' I asked Ellie. She had stopped and was listening too.

'Yes,' whispered Ellie.

'Let's go back,' I grabbed Ellie's sticky hand and gave her a tug. It was too late. Something was coming out of the box-room. A flickering light appeared and the moany voice got louder.

'Quick, *hide*.' I pulled

Ellie behind the green elephant pot and we squashed ourselves flat up against the wall.

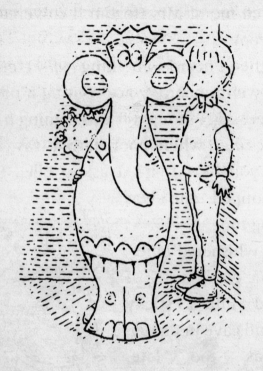

You have to hand it to Ellie, she doesn't get frightened easily. She poked her head round the pot to see what was going on.

'There's a ghost coming towards us,' she said as though it was the kind of thing you see every day.

'Don't be silly,' I whispered and glanced round the side of the pot. *She was right*!

A large figure in white was floating out of the room, followed by a flickering light. The figure was holding a book and reading from it in that moany voice that we'd heard. I had had enough.

'Let's get out of here,' I whispered, 'This place is haunted!'

But Ellie hung back. She pointed towards another door – it was Humphrey's bedroom. I couldn't believe it, that door was creaking open too. This house was stuffed full with ghosts.

'*Ellie, let's go. Come on!*' I hissed in her ear.
'*No. It's Hump-free,*' whispered Ellie.
Ellie was right. Slowly Humphrey's wide-eyed face peered out from his bedroom. He looked how I felt – scared.

'MUM!' he squeaked. 'Mum, what are you doing?'

From the shadows behind the white moany figure came the unmistakable voice of Mrs Hogbin.

'Shh, Humphrey, be quiet. We're getting rid of the ghosts.'

'She's not getting rid of them, she's collecting them,' giggled Ellie. 'Can't she see that fat one in front of her?'

'What's that?' Mrs Hogbin stopped still and listened. She must have heard Ellie. We both froze.

'It's no good, Vicar,' Mrs Hogbin said to the moany figure in white, 'I can still hear strange noises. I've been hearing them up in the attic all day *and* last night.' She shuddered and lowered her voice to a dramatic whisper, *'I think that's where they, er, live. In the attic.'*

The fat moany ghost sighed. 'Very well, Mrs Hogbin, we'll do the attic next. Do you think we could turn the lights on now?'

'Oh Vicar, don't you think the candle-light is much nicer? I think the ghosts prefer it,' said Mrs Hogbin.

'Well I don't,' said the fat moany ghost, who sounded a bit short-tempered to me. 'I can hardly see what I'm reading. I think it would be best if you turned the light on, Mrs Hogbin.'

Mrs Hogbin sounded disappointed. 'Very well, Vicar. You know best.' She blew out the candle she was holding and went to switch on the landing light.

Then she screamed, I think it was one of her best ever. It made my ears ring.

'Aah-ooOOH!' she yelled. 'The switch! It's slimy, it's – eurgh…' Then she slipped on something and crashed to the floor, taking a couple of small pots with her.

It went very quiet after that. But not for long.

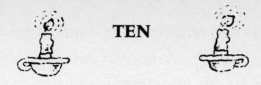

TEN

Ellie has always been nosy. All I wanted to do was to hide behind the big green elephant until everyone had gone away. But not Ellie. She turned on the torch and trotted out.

I suppose the vicar did get a bit of a shock when Ellie came out from behind the pot. I don't know what Mrs Hogbin had been telling him about the ghosts in the house, but suddenly he looked as though he believed her. First, his hand let go of the heavy black book he was carrying, then he swayed a bit and slowly slid down to the floor. There was a muffled thump as he joined Mrs Hogbin on the fluffy pink carpet.

Humphrey was all right, though. He only gasped a bit.

'Hump-free,' said Ellie happily, 'can I have my slug bucket back please?'

'Huh?' said Humphrey. He was staring at his mum and the vicar who were cluttering up the landing. Perhaps Humphrey wasn't all right after all, I thought.

'Slug bucket,' said Ellie slowly, 'I've come to get my slug bucket.' She wasn't getting through to Humphrey at all. I decided Ellie needed some help so I took a deep breath and stepped out from behind the elephant.

'Oh…' said Humphrey.

'Hello Humphrey,' I said as though I had just bumped into him down at the shops. 'How are you?'

'Um...' said Humphrey. Well, Humphrey wasn't being much use, I thought.

'Why don't you turn on the light, Humphrey?' I suggested.

'Ah...' said Humphrey and he fumbled for the light switch. That seemed to do the trick. 'Yuk!' he yelled and waggled his hand in the air.

A huge slug flew off his hand and landed on my nose. I don't think I have ever felt anything quite so revolting in all my life.

Turning the light on probably wasn't such a good idea after all. What a sight. There were slugs everywhere. The whole of the fluffy pink carpet was covered in slugs. There were slugs all over the pots, slugs climbing up the wall and a huge squashed slug stuck on bottom of Mrs Hogbin's shoe. Sitting in the corner by the green elephant was Ellie's slug bucket. It was empty.

'MY SLUGS!' yelled Ellie. 'They've escaped. Help me catch them, Hump-free.'

But Humphrey did not do what Ellie told him. He was looking at his mum and the vicar who were both still flat out on the floor.

'What shall we do about Mum?' he asked me. 'Do you think she'll wake up soon?' I looked at Mrs Hogbin. I thought I saw her eyelids flicker.

'I think she's waking up now,' I said. 'Perhaps me and Ellie ought to go home.' I really didn't want to be around when Mrs Hogbin woke up. And we *had* promised Mum that we wouldn't go near her.

Meanwhile Ellie had got her empty slug bucket and was slowly picking up the escaped slugs.

'You're very naughty slugs,' she told them. 'You've got biscuit crumbs all over you. You will have to have a bath.' Then she saw the squashed slug on the bottom of Mrs Hogbin's shoe. She let out a loud yell.

'LOOK! She's killed Frank. *She's killed Frank!*'

As if by magic, Mrs Hogbin sat up.

'Mum, Mum, are you OK?' asked

Humphrey, but she didn't answer him. She just stared at Ellie as though her worst nightmare had come true. Then she noticed the vicar who looked very comfortable on the carpet, I thought. Mrs Hogbin gasped as she took in the scene. Slugs, smashed pots, Ellie and a dead vicar. I could see that it might not look too good from her point of view.

'*Mum,*' said Humphrey again, 'are you OK?' He knelt down beside her. Mrs Hogbin stared at Humphrey as though he were another of Ellie's slugs.

'Humphrey,' she said, very quietly, 'what is that rat doing inside your jumper?'

ELEVEN

'Tell me how you found Harold again' Ellie pestered Humphrey as we sat around the fire drinking tomato soup. Ellie was not one to let a good story go to waste by only hearing it once.

'Well, when you two went home and while Mum was um, out, I spent the whole afternoon looking through every single box. But he wasn't there.'

'Trust Harold,' said Ellie happily as she cast a glance at the sleeping Harold and the sock in the cage. Harold really liked the sock so we had left it there to keep him company.

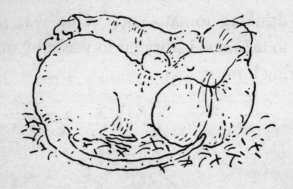

'I went and got another packet of biscuits. They were chocolate digestive.'

'Wow, lucky Harold,' said Ellie.

'Then, when I came back upstairs he was waiting for me on the top step. He just sat there cleaning his whiskers and looking at me. I think he was looking at the biscuits really. So I sat down next to him and he didn't run away.'

'He wouldn't,' said Ellie, 'not if you had a packet of chocolate digestives.'

'I got out a biscuit and started eating it. He rushed up my arm and grabbed the biscuit. Then he dived inside my jumper and ate the biscuit there.' Humphrey wriggled. 'I'm all itchy now, I've got biscuit crumbs everywhere.'

Ellie giggled. 'Why didn't you bring Harold back then?' she asked.

'I was just about to,' explained Humphrey, 'when Mum came in with the vicar, so I took Harold into my bedroom to keep him safe. It's funny,' he grinned, 'I did think the carpet was a bit squishy. But it was too dark to see all your slugs. I bet I squashed loads of them.'

'*Hump-free.* Don't be so horrid.' Ellie pulled a face. 'Well you can't have done 'cos I've counted them. Your mum squashed Frank and Eric got squished on the light switch, so there's only Molly and Fred missing.'

'Ellie, don't be silly,' I said. 'All slugs looks the same. You can't know which is which.'

'They don't and I do. So there,' Ellie retorted.

Mum came in and said, 'Humphrey, you'd better go and get your things. Would you like me to come over with you?'

'We'll go with Hump-free, won't we Hump-free?' said Ellie.

'OK,' said Humphrey. He fished around in his pocket for his key.

'Don't be long now,' said Mum.

Ellie, Humphrey and I walked out of our front gate and into his driveway. We walked up to his front door and Humphrey opened it. Then we all went into the house. It was the first time Ellie and I had ever gone into Humphrey's house through the front door.

We went upstairs and helped Humphrey pack his pyjamas and toothbrush. I noticed that when Ellie wasn't looking he stuffed a funny old teddy into his bag. Then the phone rang.

I don't know why it sounded so spooky, but it did. We all stood there looking at each other. It was an old phone and it echoed through the house: *ring ring, ring ring, ring ring.*

It was Ellie who picked it up.

'Hello,' she said, then, 'Hello? Hello, is there anyone there? Oh... ' She held out the phone as though it was a particularly nasty rattlesnake. 'Hump-free, it's your mummy,' she said.

'Hello, Mum,' said Humphrey. 'Are you feeling better now?...No, you remember, I'm staying with Ellie and Kate...Of course I'll be all right...They're not that bad Mum...Yes I'll be careful...Er, that was Ellie...She doesn't do it on purpose Mum...OK, OK, yes...Fine, yes Mum... Bye.'

Humphrey put the phone down. 'Phew,' he said.

'Where has your mummy gone?' asked Ellie.

'She's gone on a – oh, I can't remember what it's called.'

'A retreat,' I said. 'That's what it's called. The vicar's gone too. It's somewhere quiet and peaceful, like the doctor said they needed.'

'Is your mummy coming back?' asked Ellie.

'Of course she's coming back,' said Humphrey as he picked up his bag.

'Oh.' Ellie sounded disappointed.

'But not for a whole two weeks, Ellie,' I said. 'Humphrey and you and me are going to have a great time, aren't we Humphrey?'

Humphrey grinned as we locked up his front door and went back to our flat. 'You bet,' he said.

And we did, we had a really great time. We played up in the top flat and we could go anywhere we liked in Humphrey's house too. We didn't tell Mum about the secret door. Well, you know what grown-ups are like, they never really understand about things like that.

Humphrey discovered that he *liked* slugs. He stopped Ellie washing them in the bath and helped her pick the biscuit crumbs off them. Then he sprayed them all with water because they were drying out. I couldn't bear to look. Humphrey helped Ellie finish off her slug holiday village too. It looked

completely revolting to me but here's a picture of it so that you can see for yourself just how disgusting it was.

The only boring bit was when Mum made us all sit down and make get well soon cards for Mrs Hogbin. Still, I expect they made her feel much better, although I'm not so sure about Ellie's card. I expect you can guess what Ellie drew on the front of her card. That's right, a big, fat slug.

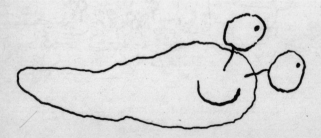